VIVA HEATHER!
by Sheri Cooper Sinykin

Illustrations by
Richard Lauter

Spot Illustrations by
Rich Grote and Catherine Huerta

MagicAttic
Club

MAGIC ATTIC PRESS

For more information contact:
Book Editor, Magic Attic Press, 866 Spring Street,
P.O. Box 9722, Portland, ME 04104-5022

First Edition
Printed in the United States of America
1 2 3 4 5 6 7 8 9 10

Magic Attic Club is a registered trademark.

Betsy Gould, Publisher
Marva Martin, Art Director
Robin Haywood, Managing Editor

Edited by Judit Bodnar
Designed by Susi Oberhelman

ISBN 1-57513-068-8

Magic Attic Club books are printed on acid-free, recycled paper.

As members of the
MAGIC ATTIC CLUB,
we promise to
be best friends,
share all of our adventures in the attic,
use our imaginations,
have lots of fun together,
and remember—the real magic is in us.

Alison   Keisha

Heather   Megan

Contents

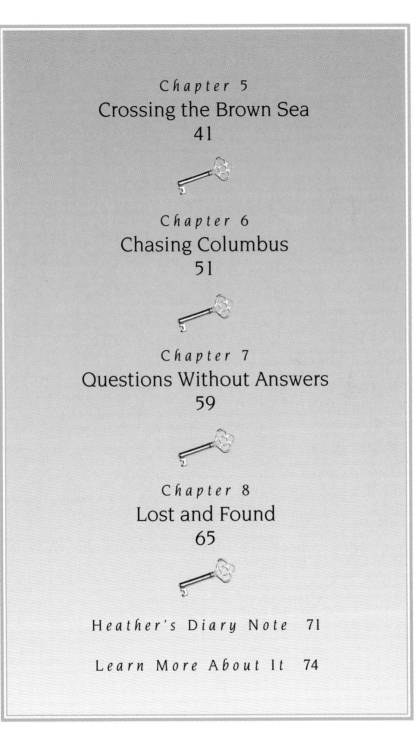

GRANDMA'S SURPRISE

eather sat on her bed and opened the small velvet box. "Oh, Grandma!" she gasped. "It's beautiful! Will you help me put it on?"

"With pleasure." Grandma Hardin's fingers tickled the back of Heather's neck as she fastened the chain. "Wear it in good health." When she positioned the gold charm in front, her dark eyes shone. "That's Hebrew for—"

"*Chai*, right?" Heather cut in. "It's almost like the letter that means 'take half' on the Chanukah dreidel."

Her grandmother nodded. "Actually, the word *chai* has two letters, and it means 'life', or the number eighteen. But it's also the beginning of Haya, your Hebrew name." She kissed Heather's cheek. "Happy Passover, dear."

"Thank you, Grandma!" Heather said, hugging her. "I'm so glad you could come this year."

"Thanks to my son the pilot." Grandma Hardin beamed with pride. "I've got another surprise, too, but . . ." Her voice drifted off, and her eyes watered strangely.

"But what?" begged Heather. "Tell me."

"Not till the second seder," her grandmother said.

"Why not the first one? Why do I have to wait *two* nights?"

"There's always so much commotion at Aunt Rachel's. And this is one package I wouldn't want getting broken."

So it was something fragile. Heather wracked her brain with guesses. "Just give me a clue, okay? Pretty please?"

Grandma Hardin smiled. "How much do you know about your Spanish heritage?"

"We're Spanish? No way." Hardin certainly didn't sound like a Hispanic last name. Heather couldn't believe that her parents had never mentioned this before. Was it possible that they didn't know?

"We're Sephardim, actually. Spanish Jews. Don't they teach you anything in that temple school of yours?" Grandma Hardin peered at Heather over her glasses.

Heather avoided her grandmother's gaze. Maybe her teachers had tried, but she probably wasn't listening. It was hard to get excited about the long, sad history of the Jewish people. What was done was done. Why did they have to keep dredging up the past every year—especially at Passover? That was the worst. While everyone else was hunting for colored Easter eggs and eating candy, Jewish kids were hunting for matzohs and eating strange-smelling foods that made them remember . . . and cry.

"Well," Grandma Hardin said, "the Hardins—or should

I say harDEENs? That's Spanish for 'garden', dear—go way back before Columbus even. Your grandfather's family settled in southern Spain, a place called Granada. Did you know that means 'pomegranate'?"

Heather shook her head and glanced at her watch. It sounded like her grandmother was going to ramble on for some time, and Heather still had to write spelling sentences and do two pages of story problems before bedtime. She listened politely while her grandmother explained that a pomegranate was a strange fruit filled with juicy red seeds. Then she cleared her throat. "This is interesting, really, Grandma, but I still have a lot of homework to do," Heather said at last.

"But I was just getting to the part about the Hardins pretending to be gypsies. Those were scary days, Heather. Are you sure your religious-school teacher never talked about the Inquisition? The time in Spanish history when the rulers wanted everyone to belong to their faith or else they'd be killed?"

Heather shrugged, then turned toward the math book sitting on her desk. "Is it okay if you tell me this tomorrow?" she asked.

"Tomorrow it is," Grandma Hardin said. "Or as they say in Spain—"

"*Mañana!*" Heather cut in. Now the word felt strange

on her tongue. If things had been different, Spanish would have been her native language.

On the way home from school the next day with her best friends, Heather felt for the shape of the *chai* charm beneath her T-shirt. School wasn't the best place to wear jewelry you didn't want to lose, Heather knew. Especially on gym days. Keeping it hidden had seemed a good idea.

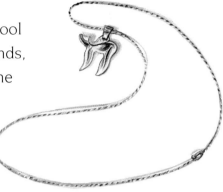

"Heather, is that your grandma?" Megan Ryder asked, pointing to the stout woman who was waving at them from the Hardins' driveway.

Heather nodded and quickly pulled the charm out so her grandmother would be sure to see it. "She got here yesterday."

"What did you tell her about us?" Keisha Vance raised one eyebrow and grinned.

"Not *everything*, I hope," Alison McCann added.

"Not about the Magic Attic Club," Heather said, "if that's what you mean."

"Good." Alison slipped her arm around Heather's shoulder. "Not that we really thought you'd tell or anything."

Even if she had, Heather suspected that no one would understand the Magic Attic Club except her three friends and their neighbor, Ellie Goodwin, a music teacher who had invited them to play in her amazing attic. Heather only knew that as soon as the girls tried on costumes from the old steamer trunk up there and then gazed into Ellie's tall gilded mirror, they suddenly embarked on astounding adventures.

"Ah, finally I get to meet your friends, Heather!" Grandma Hardin opened her arms as if to give the four girls a group hug. "Come. You'll sample Jenna's *charoseth.*"

Alison and Keisha looked confused, but Megan whispered that *charoseth* was some kind of Passover food.

"So you girls have never been to a seder?" Grandma Hardin asked as she led the way into the house.

Heather brought up the rear. Next thing you know, she thought, Grandma will be inviting them. Heather could imagine nothing more embarrassing than watching her best friends suffer politely through that endless meal of prayers and stories about the Jews being slaves in Egypt. Her cheeks grew warm at the thought as she took the girls' jackets, then followed them into the kitchen, where her older sister was already at work.

"You see here?" Grandma Hardin said, indicating the contents of Jenna's wooden chopping bowl. "That's *charoseth.*"

Alison make a face at the
brownish paste of finely
chopped apples and
walnuts, even though it was
fragrant with cinnamon and a
splash of Passover wine.

"It tastes better than it looks," Heather said.

"Can we try some?" asked Keisha. Jenna politely
offered a sample to each of them.

"Heather's right," Alison said. "It does taste better
than it looks." She smiled at Heather, then, cocking her
head, stared at Heather's necklace. "That's new, isn't it?"
she asked. "It's really cool."

The others gathered around to admire it, too, and
Heather told them all about the Hebrew charm. "Come
on," she whispered. "Let's get out of here before they put
us to work. You want to go to Ellie's?"

Megan, Alison, and Keisha nodded eagerly and made
a rush for the front door. Heather's hand was on the knob
when her grandmother's call stopped her cold.

"Girls? You running off? How'd you like to come to
seder here tomorrow night? I think you'd all find it quite
interesting. Don't you, Heather?"

Whatever the truth was, it made Heather squirm. She
could do nothing more than nod weakly.

Chapter TWO

PEANUT BUTTER
AND
JELLY BLUES

 eather wished she'd had a chance to tell her friends that a seder wasn't nearly as exciting as her grandmother made it sound. Before she could stop them, they'd gone home to check with their parents, promising to call later.

All through her Aunt's seder on the first night of Passover, Heather kept trying to imagine how Megan, Alison, and Keisha would react the next evening to the second seder. No doubt they'd be starving by the time the

Passover story was finally over. Would her mother, like her aunt, insist that everyone eat enough bitter herbs to make tears come? Probably. And Heather was certain that the girls would think it was crazy to open the front door for the prophet Elijah so he could drink from an extra cup of wine.

By the time the Hardins got home, the answering machine was beeping double time. Heather raced to play the messages, half hoping her friends couldn't come. Instead, she found three cheerful acceptances. Hiding her disappointment from her grandmother, she said good night and went to bed.

Alone in the dark, Heather's thoughts raced fast-forward to tomorrow's seder. What would Alison, Keisha, and Megan think of dipping parsley in salt water, flicking ten drops of wine on a plate, and playing hide-and-seek with a matzoh? Everything about the Passover meal was so strange and embarrassing. The more Heather thought about it, the more her stomach began to hurt. If only there were some way to uninvite them . . .

When her alarm clock buzzed the next morning, Heather rolled over with a groan. She didn't feel like getting up. As a matter of fact, she was certain she was

coming down with something.
The stomach flu, maybe.

The next thing she knew, her
mother was calling her for
breakfast—and she was still in
bed! "Heather's not even up yet,"
Jenna yelled on her way downstairs.

Hunger rumbled in Heather's stomach as she threw
the covers back and reached for her robe. Moments later
her mother came in. "Get up, honey. Hurry now. Didn't
your alarm go off?" she asked.

"It did," Heather said, "but I don't feel so good."

Mrs. Hardin touched Heather's forehead. "No fever."

"It's my stomach." As if on cue, it grumbled loudly.

Her mother smiled. "Nothing a little breakfast won't
cure," she said gently. "You're probably just excited about
tonight. Once you get going, I'm sure you'll be fine."

Heather sighed. "Okay," she said at last, and headed
for the bathroom.

"I'll put your lunch by the front door," her mother
called, "so you don't forget it."

Great, Heather thought glumly. She knew from
past experience what she'd find in her paper sack. One
look at that sandwich—and her friends' faces—and
she'd be sick for sure.

"Hey, Heather!" Alison stood up and waved. "Over here."

Cradling four square cartons against her stomach, Heather wove her way across the crowded lunchroom toward her friends. It was her turn to go through the milk line for them all, and their turn to save seats. Keisha was already chomping on an apple. Megan was laying her food out neatly as she always did.

When Heather sat down, Alison pulled her own sandwich out and inspected it. "Yuck. What's this?"

Megan frowned. "Tongue, maybe?"

"No way. Mom would never make me taste something that could taste *me*," Alison said indignantly.

Megan and Keisha giggled. Heather managed only a thin smile and didn't open her lunch bag.

"Come on, Heather," Alison urged. "See what you've got. Want to trade?"

Heather stalled. "Uh, I'm not very hungry, and anyway, my stomach's been bugging me all day."

"It's the spelling test," Keisha said knowingly. "Nerves."

"Whatever you've got in there, I'll eat it." Alison grinned. "It's got to be better than tongue."

"Okay, you asked for it." Heather pulled out a plastic sandwich bag splotched with peanut butter and grape jelly. The fillings oozed from between two squares of matzoh. "Change your mind?"

Alison wrinkled her nose. Megan and Keisha exchanged a look of surprise. "What *is* that?" Alison asked at last.

"Peanut butter and jelly on matzoh," Heather said glumly, "instead of bread made with flour. Because of Passover."

"Yeah, but—" Keisha began.

Heather cut her off. "It's to remember how fast the Jews had to leave Egypt. They didn't even have time to let their bread rise." There. At least she'd learned something at temple school.

"Oh." Alison nodded. "Well, I guess we *can't* trade then, can we?"

Heather shook her head as a couple of other kids at their table made dumb jokes like "What's the matter, Heather? Is your cracker sandwich cracked?" She couldn't bring herself to eat anything but her oranges. "I—I don't know for sure," she said at last, "but I could be getting the flu. I wonder if you guys should still come over tonight."

"Oh, Heather." Keisha, plainly disappointed, clicked her tongue. Alison and Megan frowned.

"I know—why don't you see how you feel later?" Megan suggested. "Call and let us know."

"Are you sure?"

The three girls all nodded.

"Okay, then," Heather said. "Let's see how the rest of the day goes. I'll call you."

Keisha, Megan, and Alison held their fingers up and crossed them. "Here's hoping for a speedy recovery," Alison said. "Ask your grandmother. Maybe she knows some special remedy."

They all looked so concerned that Heather felt a bit guilty. She knew that she wouldn't find a cure in any of her grandmother's medicine bottles for what really ailed her. But she might in Ellie's attic.

Chapter Three

A GYPSY
IN THE PALACE

When Heather returned from school, her mother and grandmother had gone shopping. Jenna was setting the table in the dining room. Except during Passover, Heather never even saw the fancy china, newly polished silverware, and linen napkins.

"Is it okay if I go to Ellie's?" she asked her sister.

Jenna nodded. "But don't be gone long."

"Am I ever?" Heather grinned, then hurried across the street to Ellie Goodwin's stately Victorian house. The older woman was out front, raking her lawn. "Hi, Ellie!" Heather waved. "Need some help?"

Ellie shook her head. "Thank you, dear, but I'm almost done here. Why don't you go on up to the attic and have some fun?"

Heather needed no urging. Claiming the golden key from its little silver box in the entry hall, she raced upstairs. The now familiar attic, with its mahogany wardrobe, trunk full of costumes, and tall gilded mirror, spread before her like a banquet. Which outfit should she try on today? Riffling through the selection, she was amazed at how many new ones there seemed to be since the last time she'd looked.

A ruffled gypsy outfit caught Heather's eye. Hadn't her grandmother said something about the Hardins being Spanish gypsies? Heather wished that she'd been paying better attention before.

Hurriedly she kicked off her sneakers and jeans and slipped into the sandals and flouncy skirt. Next she put on the blouse, vest, and lacy shawl. Tucking a red silk rose behind her ear, she stepped up to the mirror to admire her new outfit.

Imagine! A Jewish gypsy! Heather raised her arms, pretending to hold castanets. Then, stomping her feet, she turned in a slow circle. Her skirt spun out like cresting waves. Faster and faster she whirled, until at last, dizzy, she stopped to look at her reflection. Her image swam, and she blinked hard, trying to bring it into focus.

Ellie's looking glass had shrunk into a small round hand mirror. Beautiful metalwork surrounded the glass. It stood on a massive wooden chest in a colorfully tiled room. Behind her, water—or perhaps perfume, because it gave off a definite bouquet—trickled into a raised bathing pool. Heather drew her breath in sharply. What if this were someone's private chamber? She quickly backed out of the room.

Beneath an archway, Heather stopped to marvel at its intricate carvings. Sunlight filtered through, dappling the tile floor. Where could she be? She glanced about, but found no clue.

Footsteps echoed from somewhere nearby. Heather turned and fled down a long open corridor. At last she came to a courtyard. A fountain burbled on the backs of twelve stone lions. Each one spewed water from his mouth. Fascinated, Heather tiptoed closer to investigate.

"E*spére un momento!*"

The deep voice startled Heather almost as much as the fact that she'd understood what it said: "Wait a moment." She reeled about and froze. A young, dark-haired man was hurrying toward her. He was dressed in clothes right out of a history book. His eyebrows made one hard line across his forehead.

"*Por qué estás aquí, chica?*"—"Why are you here, girl?"— he asked in that strange language Heather somehow understood.

"I-I don't know," Heather said. But the words came out as "*No lo sé.*" A shiver raced along her spine. No matter how many times she traveled on adventures through Ellie's mirror, she was never quite prepared for the amazing abilities she seemed to bring with her.

"How did you get past the guards, then?" the young man asked.

Guards? Heather glanced about, but saw no sign of them. Where *was* she? What year was this?

"Come," he said, and seized her wrist. "You do not

belong here in the Court of the Lions, or in any part of the Alhambra, for that matter. This has been Their Royal Majesties' palace since January. You must go."

Heather resisted his efforts to lead her out. "That is the problem exactly," she said in his language. "*Perdida*."—"I am lost."—"Please, can you help me?"

"Well, that depends," he said, "on who you are."

Heather didn't like the haughty way he was looking at her. She straightened her blouse and drew herself up tall. "My name is Heather," she replied. "Heather Hardin." She pronounced her last name harDEEN, the same way her grandmother had.

"You say Jardin?" The young man eyed her suspiciously. "I believe I know that name. Your family has had business here at the Alhambra, *sí*?"

"I-I'm not sure," Heather stammered, trying to mask her surprise that he recognized her last name.

The young man shook his head. "I seem to recall an astronomer, a student of Zacuto, but he was . . ." Before Heather could stop him, he reached for her *chai* necklace. He didn't jerk it free, but simply studied it closely. His expression softened. "Ah. *Comprendo*. You are a Jew, *sí*? You are looking for your family?"

"*Sí*, but I don't know where—"

"You are in grave danger here," he said, his voice

26

suddenly urgent and low. "Time is running out. You and your people must accept the Faith of Their Royal Majesties or leave Spain."

Heather frowned. Something about his words sounded familiar, except for the last part about leaving Spain. Still, that was better than the part that echoed in her head: *or they'd be killed.*

"But . . . why?" she whispered. "And why should I believe you?"

"Forgive me. My name is Carlos Nuñez. I am at your service."—"*Me llamo Carlos Nuñez, a sus órdenes.*"—"My father is counsel to the King, one of only a few Jewish advisers to stay and accept the Faith."

"Then you're Jewish, too?"

"Shhh!" Carlos glanced furtively about. "I am a *converso,* a convert. But in my heart . . ." He didn't finish his thought. "The decree was issued in March, and people have had only these past few months to make their choice. But now the deadline draws near. All Jews must be gone by midnight on August the second. Or else." He drew one finger across his throat.

Heather swallowed hard as another word—this one clearly in Grandma Hardin's voice—rang in her ears: *Inquisition.*

"Believe me, Heather," Carlos went on, "if King

27

Ferdinand or Queen Isabella were to find you here now . . ."

"Queen Isabella? *The* Queen Isabella?" Heather's eyes went wide. "The one who sent Christopher Columbus—"

"How do *you* know of Columbus?" Carlos interrupted. Heather shrugged vaguely, and he continued. "In less than a fortnight, he sails west from Palos for the Indies, if indeed the world is round as he claims. I am to take a message to him from Their Majesties."

"You? Oh, Carlos, that's so exciting!" Obviously Columbus had not yet discovered the New World, but he was about to, which put the year at 1492. Heather was relieved that Carlos hadn't questioned her slip of the tongue about Columbus. Maybe he'd let her go with him to see the famous explorer—wouldn't that be some adventure to tell the rest of the Magic Attic Club? "When do you leave?" she asked.

"In the morning."

"May I come—"

Without warning, Carlos clapped a hand over her mouth and practically dragged her from the patio. Footsteps! Mouthing the words, "Follow me!" he rushed her into the shadows of the delicate, scalloped arcades and slender columns.

Racing after him through a maze of hallways and hedged gardens, Heather's heart pounded wildly. Her side ached, but she saw the fear in Carlos's eyes and pressed on. At last a fortress wall blocked their escape. No matter which way she turned, there was a watchtower—and a guard inside.

Hurriedly, Carlos draped Heather's shawl over her head and tied the ends around her neck. "You must hide that," he whispered, indicating her *chai*. "Our very lives depend on it."

Chapter Four

SEEK AND HIDE

 re you a good actress?"
Carlos didn't wait for a reply.
"You'd better be. Go along with
whatever I say now," he warned as
he and Heather approached an
imposing gate. "Close your eyes
and let me lead you."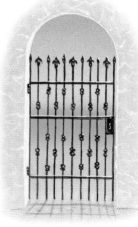

Heather obeyed, too
frightened to ask questions. Her

sandal caught on a flagstone, and she would have stumbled were it not for Carlos's firm grip on her arm.

"*Buenas tardes*. Good afternoon, Señor Nuñez," a deep voice boomed. "What business have you with this gypsy? Why is she here?"

"*Es nada más que una ciega*"—"It's merely a blind girl"— Carlos replied. "How she came to wander in the palace, I do not know. But I am returning her to the caves at Sacromonte, where she belongs."

The other man only grunted. As Carlos hustled Heather along, she heard the distinct hiss of spittle hitting the path behind her and cringed.

Carlos patted her arm. "It could have gone much worse," he said gently. "Open your eyes now and come along."

The road fell off sharply. Heather glanced back up the hill to the royal palace, the Alhambra. "What's Sacromonte?" she asked. "Where are we going?"

"To the mountain where the gypsies live. It is a long walk, but if my information is correct, you may indeed find your family there."

My family! Heather thought. Her grandmother had said the Hardins had lived as gypsies. But was it really possible to find them, especially now, with all that was going on? For their sake, Heather hoped that they'd already escaped to safety. For her own, she couldn't help wondering whether Carlos was right and she would meet them soon. Despite the fierce afternoon heat, she shivered with a strange mixture of fear and excitement. "How can I ever thank you, Carlos?"

"Save your thanks until you are safe. These are dangerous times. Trust no one. We cannot be too careful."

The road to the gypsy caves climbed a steep mountain slope opposite the Alhambra. Clumps of fig trees and cacti and prickly pear grew along the way, but they offered little shade. Heather was glad that Carlos had stopped at the marketplace for some bread, cheese, and water, which hung from his shoulder in a bota, a leather bag.

The sun beat a relentless path across the sky, but Heather and Carlos pressed on, refusing to rest. There were so many things she wanted to ask him. Why did the Jews have to leave Spain? Grandma Hardin hadn't explained anything about that, though maybe Heather's temple-school teacher had. What if Carlos failed to find her family? Then she'd keep trying on her own, Heather decided. But what if he offered to take her to see Columbus? Why was he risking his safety to help her anyway?

So many questions. Until they were safe from unseen listeners, however, she dared not speak.

"It's not much farther," Carlos said at last.

Heather's eyes grew wide at the sight ahead: Dark mouths of caves, too many to count, yawned from the hillside. Rag-clad children, pigs, and goats wandered outside. Several women were draping wet clothing on the rocks to dry.

Carlos approached a man who sat in the dirt eating an orange. "Excuse me, señor. Do you know the *familia* Jardin?" he asked.

The man shrugged.

Carlos took Heather's hand and went from person to person, asking about her family. But the answer was always the same.

"They don't trust you," Heather said finally. "You can see it in their eyes. "Maybe it's your fancy clothes—or that we're both strangers."

"I believe you're right." Carlos sighed. "But I am sure there are Jews here, living as gypsies. I have it on good authority."

"Let me try asking by myself then. At least I appear to be one of them."

"What harm can it do? Shall I wait for you here?"

Heather nodded and started off toward another cave. A thin dark-haired boy came tripping out. He collided with Heather, then collapsed at her feet and began wailing as if she had struck him.

"My goodness!" Heather knelt to comfort him, he was carrying on so. "There, there. It's just a little dirt." As she dusted him off with her shawl, another boy and a woman hurried out of the cave. Heather said to the woman. "Are you his mother? I'm sure he's not hurt."

The boy blinked up at Heather. Suddenly, his eyes grew wide. "Mamá, mira!"—"Mother, look!"

Heather's hand flew to the spot where he was pointing. But it was too late. Even a child knew that wearing a *chai* meant trouble—for all of them. Would they turn her in? "Please, señora . . ." Heather began.

But the woman cut her off with a sharp snap of her fingers. "Hurry! Inside!"

Before Heather could call out for Carlos, the woman was hustling her into the dark cave. Heather blinked, wishing her eyes would adjust. But the few pieces of furniture—a table and some stools—remained shadows. "W-What are you going to do to me?" she asked. Should she mention that she had a protector waiting just outside?

"I am going to hide you, of course," the woman responded, her voice but a whisper. "With your permission."

Heather's jaw dropped. Were these people Jewish? Words failed her, and the woman filled the awkward silence with introductions. Her name, she said, was Leah Vargas and her sons Isaac and David were four and six. At this, Heather raised her eyebrows in surprise. She had thought they might be twins, since the skinny older boy was as short as his brother. And yes, the woman admitted, answering Heather's silent question, they were Jews, too. "But we practice in secret," she whispered. "No one must know."

Heather finally managed to get her own name out and to ask, "Do you know the *familia* Jardin then?"

"Sí, but—"

"But that's wonderful!" Heather hadn't realized until that instant just how she much she really wanted to meet them.

Señora Vargas shook her head. "No. I am afraid it is not. They have already left."

"Left? When? For where?" The questions exploded from Heather, and her voice rose dangerously.

"*Cálmate, niña,*" the woman said.—"Calm yourself, girl."

"But I can't! Don't you understand? I have to find

them." Heather rushed from the cave, calling for Carlos.

He came at once. Immediately, he retied her shawl to cover the necklace. "Who saw it? Are you all right?"

Heather nodded, grabbed his hand, and fairly dragged him into the Vargas's cave. Isaac and David retreated behind their mother's skirt. Señora Vargas stood defiantly, her hands on her hips. Even so, Heather noticed, the woman's chin was trembling.

"Don't worry, señora," Heather said. "Carlos is a friend. He is—was—one of us. We can trust him."

"You have my word as a gentleman," Carlos added. "I am only trying to help the girl find her family."

Señora Vargas's expression softened. "The *familia* Jardin left for Sevilla only two days ago. If God wills it, they will sail for the north of Africa, then on to Turkey, where they will be safe."

"Only two days, Carlos!" Heather clapped her hands. "Maybe we can catch them."

"We? But I must leave tomorrow for Palos harbor, remember?"

"Yes, but"—Heather squeezed her eyes shut, trying to picture the map of Spain she'd made for that explorers unit in school last year—"isn't Sevilla on the way?"

Carlos nodded. "I suppose that could work."

But Señora Vargas bristled at Heather's question. "You

IBERIAN PENINSULA
ca. 1492

FRANCE

NAVARRE

ARAGON

C A S T I L E

P O R T U G A L

Toledo

Valencia

Palos

Sevilla

Granada

A N D A L U S

M O R O C C O

are a young girl, and Carlos is not a relative. Travel together without a *dueña*?—a chaperone?—*Imposible!*"

"Then come with us," Heather insisted. "All of you. Get out of Spain. Before it's too late. I'm sure we can help you." She waited for Carlos to protest, but he appeared actually to be considering the idea.

"Can Papa come, too?" Isaac asked.

Señora Vargas chewed her lip but did not reply. Carlos bent forward to tousle Isaac's hair, and Heather beamed him a silent plea. After a moment, he straightened up and cleared his throat. "Forgive me for saying so, señora. But if I know of your hiding place, surely others will, too. How safe can it be to stay here?"

"How safe can it be to make such a journey?" Señora Vargas sighed as if the very thought overwhelmed her.

"But he will be carrying a message from the King and Queen," Heather added. "That should help, shouldn't it?"

"Indeed!" Señora Vargas's tone brightened. In the dim light she reached for Heather's hand and gave it a little squeeze. "David," she said, turning to the older boy, "go get Papa. And hurry. We have much to discuss." She glanced about the cave, then murmured almost to herself, "And much to do if Papa says yes."

Chapter Five

CROSSING THE BROWN SEA

Abraham Vargas agreed at once and even loaned Carlos a mule to hasten his return to the Alhambra to get travel supplies and the royal message for Columbus. After a meager meal of figs, dried meat, and bread, Heather helped the boys and their mother bundle their few possessions for the journey. She felt vaguely guilty for having eaten bread, but it wasn't Passover here, after all, and she had to eat *something*.

"Mama," David said, "don't forget the vase."

His mother smiled. "*Nunca, hijo.*"—"Never, son." From a niche in the wall of the cave she gingerly retrieved a squat, muddy-colored urn. It was the ugliest vase Heather had ever seen. Still, Señora Vargas handled it with the same care that Heather's own mother gave fine china. She asked Heather to bring her a shawl and some straw from the floor, then proceeded to wrap and swaddle it like a beloved newborn.

"Enough now," Señor Vargas said. "Let's join the others for some singing and dancing." He handed Heather a tambourine. "Come. Who knows what fate will bring us tomorrow? We must celebrate hope and new friends tonight."

And so Heather and the Vargas family joined the gypsies around the campfire under the starry summer sky. Their songs filled the night with cries and wails that seemed to  come from some deep place in each singer's soul. Somehow they reminded Heather of the prayer songs of the bent old men in her synagogue. Castanets clicked to the strains of guitars, and before long dancers were on their feet, whirling and clapping to the music. Isaac joined in, though his older brother clung to Heather. Soon, however, she, too, felt the music inside her, and spun about with Isaac to the gypsies' song.

Much later, despite itchy straw bedding in the musty cave, Heather slept. Morning brought Carlos back, with his horse-drawn wagon, supplies, and the mule. The boys acted as if they were embarking on a great adventure. But when their parents handed Carlos the last bundles, Heather could read the fear and uncertainty in their eyes.

"You'd all best ride in back," Carlos said, "and keep well hidden. I've a letter of safe passage from Their Majesties, but it will go badly for all of us if I am caught helping Jews."

As the Vargas family climbed aboard, Carlos gave Heather a loose hooded robe, insisting she wear it. "Be certain to cover your face if we are stopped," he said.

The fabric was as rough as burlap, and Heather knew that once the sun climbed higher, it was going to be uncomfortably hot. But she said nothing. Whatever it took to keep herself safe and to find her family, she would do.

At last the wagon jostled away down the hill and turned west toward Sevilla. Heather realized, as the day wore on, that nothing in her life had prepared her for such a journey. The oppressive heat, the cramped conditions in the back of the wagon, the need to hide at the sight of other travelers all made her as cross and restless as Isaac and David, who squabbled endlessly and vied for their parents' attention.

Señora Vargas told the boys stories until her voice tired. Then Heather took over, teaching them cat's cradle with a piece of string. Isaac learned more quickly than his older brother. David soon lay down, complaining that he didn't feel well, but Isaac kept playing long after Heather wanted to stop.

"Maybe the heat's getting to him," Heather said. "He needs to drink more water." But David did more sleeping than drinking. Heather took it on herself to rouse him now and then to offer him sips.

Señora Vargas cast Heather a grateful smile as Isaac at last settled back against her and drowsed off. "You are a good girl. I cannot imagine how the *familia* Jardin could leave behind such a treasure!"

"I'm a distant relation," Heather hedged, then added truthfully, "and they didn't know I was coming."

The travelers passed the first night at an inn. Heather's bed was flea-ridden, and in the morning her arms and legs were pocked with red bites. The boys had fared no better. "When are we going to get there?" they kept asking as the trip dragged on.

The arid countryside lurched past. Olive trees stood

like soldiers all the way to the horizon. As the wagon bumped along the dirt road, one day ran into the next. Once an official galloped up in a cloud of dust. Heather and the Vargas family dove for cover beneath the blankets and straw. But the man, satisfied with Carlos's letter from Their Majesties, wished him godspeed and swiftly sent him on his way.

Sometimes they camped with other travelers, some sick, all weary. Heather overheard whispers in the night: "What day is it?" "What month?" She wondered whether these strangers, too, were trying to flee Spain before the deadline. Even without a calendar she knew that time was getting short.

At last Carlos pointed out the Giralda tower on the banks of the Guadalquivir River. The minaret seemed to stand watch over sun-bleached Sevilla. "Look at all the ships!" he cried. "We're not too late."

Heather stood up in the wagon. At the sight of so many masts and sails and people, her pulse quickened. How would she find her family?

Señora Vargas helped her husband extract handfuls of *maravedis* from the lining of his boot. It looked like a fortune in coins. Finally Carlos stopped and secured the wagon near the throng of fellow travelers, all pushing and pressing to get closer to the ships. "Papa will go buy us passage," Señora Vargas explained to the children. "We must hurry and unload our things."

Heather tapped Carlos's arm. "But what about—"

"You stay with Leah and the boys." Carlos's voice had a new all-business snap, and Heather noticed that he kept scanning the crowd. "I will check with the sailing master about your family. Do not go anywhere. I will be back."

Heather watched Señor Vargas and Carlos head off. A lump rose in her throat as they melted into the crowd. Don't be silly, she told herself, of course

they'll be back. She pushed the fear from her mind and helped Señora Vargas assemble the family's belongings while Isaac and David chased about nearby. By the time their father returned, they were both begging to be carried down to the pier.

Señor Vargas reached into his boot and pulled out a necklace that jangled with old coins. "If you had not come to our little cave, who knows what fate might have met us there," he said to Heather. "Please accept this with our thanks."

"Oh, but I couldn't. Wherever you go, you might need it. For the boys."

"No. Please. Leah and I insist." He placed the strand around her neck, then tucked it safely beneath her robe.

"Thank you," Heather said. Though she was still uncomfortable accepting such generosity, she feared that refusing it might hurt their feelings. "At least let me help with the boys." She handed the carefully bundled vase to Señora Vargas. "Come here, David. Hop on."

"You're supposed to wait for Carlos," the boy whispered as he clung to her shoulders and wrapped his legs about her waist.

"It's all right." The cloak's hood flopped over Heather's face and hid her reassuring smile. "We can meet him down there."

"Hurry now," Señor Vargas said tersely. "I don't like the looks of this crowd. Let's get through it and go on aboard."

Heather frowned, unsure what he meant. "Me, too?" she asked, struggling to keep up.

"Sí, of course," his wife replied. "It is the first of August. It is not safe for you to stay."

"But what if Carlos can't find my family?"

Señora Vargas looked at her husband. He nodded quickly. "Then you will go with us," she said firmly.

Before Heather could protest, Señora Vargas was charging after her husband and Isaac. "Hey!" Heather called. "Wait for me." With David on her back, it was hard to keep up. Besides that, she kept stepping on the hem of her robe. "Excuse me," she said as she bumped into someone.

A chant started at the far edge of the crowd. Heather couldn't make it out. And she couldn't see Leah Vargas—or even Isaac on her husband's shoulders—anymore, either. Her stomach tightened. The crowd pressed close about her, pushing and surging in waves. "David," she called up to the boy, "do you see them?"

"Sí. Put me down. I will show you."

She stopped and he slid from her back, then darted ahead into the sea of people. As she chased after him, the chanting swelled, its words now distinct. "Jews! Jews! Jews!"

Heather swallowed hard. She couldn't see David, couldn't see *any* of them now. She tried to call out, but their names stuck in her throat. Carlos! Where was Carlos? Pushing her hood back, she turned, frantic to find a familiar face.

Sudden pain exploded in the back of her head.

Confused, she whirled about in time to see several rocks sail toward the teeming gangway. Her head throbbed dully. As she touched the spot, she winced, then pulled her hand back. It was covered with blood.

Chapter

Six

CHASING COLUMBUS

eather's knees went weak at the sight of her own blood, but she forced herself to think clearly. If she fell, she'd be trampled. And if she didn't find the Vargases, she'd be left behind. Yet trying to escape the angry mob was as hopeless as running through quicksand. Imagine what would happen if they discovered she was Jewish!

Checking to make sure her *chai* was well hidden, Heather burrowed back under her hood. Helmeted officials on horseback were ordering the people to disperse. Heather

wondered whether she should ask for their
help, but she remembered Carlos's warning: *Trust no
one*. With a sudden shudder she wondered, Does that
include Carlos?

The crowd surged forward, taking Heather with it. Her
feet left the ground. And now someone was grabbing her!
She screamed as strong arms pulled her free of the
chanting peasants.

"Shhh!" The man clamped a hand over her mouth. "It's
me, Carlos!" he hissed.

Relieved, Heather slumped against him. "I-I thought
you'd left. I thought—"

"Come on. We've got to get out of here." Carlos skirted
the crowd, pulling Heather by the hand.

"But what about my family? And the Vargases?"

Carlos stopped and faced her. "They're safe. I saw
them board. But there's no record of any *familia* Jardin,
Heather."

Her lip quivered. "Are you sure?"

Carlos only shrugged. "Perhaps they gave another
name. Or sailed on another ship. I'm truly sorry."

"But . . ." Heather turned toward the river. Travelers
kept streaming up the gangway and onto the deck. Sails
began to billow and dance above them. She strained to
catch a glimpse of Isaac or David. "What about me?"

"I can take you as far as Palos, fifty miles or so," Carlos answered. "But after that, I dare not risk another day in your company." He started toward the wagon, and Heather hurried along behind.

"But why?" she blurted out, catching his arm. "Why risk it at all?"

Carlos's eyes softened as he adjusted the hood about her face. "For love of my little *prima*, my cousin," he said. "You remind me of her."

"Did she . . . die?"

Carlos shook his head. "At least, I hope not. She and her parents fled to Holland, but I doubt I shall ever see her again."

"I-I'm sorry."

"Sí, I am, too." Carlos turned abruptly to inspect his horse. As he adjusted the harness, the Vargas's mule, tethered at the rear, brayed softly.

Without a word, Heather slipped around to the far side of the wagon to comfort him. When she was sure that no one was watching, she scrambled up and hid beneath the straw.

"We're here, Heather. Wake up!"

Heather blinked up at a starry sky. The stench of dead fish filled the air. She struggled to remember where she was. Oh, yes. With Carlos. Chasing Columbus. "What day is it? Are we in time?"

"See for yourself."

Hurriedly, she slipped her robe on again, then scrambled to her feet in the back of the wagon. Anchored in the harbor were three small ships—the *Pinta*, the *Niña*, and the *Santa Maria*, she supposed. A strong-looking man with snowy hair stood on shore, directing others into rowboats. Though Heather could not hear his exact words, she had the feeling that he was rushing them, that he was worried about the late hour.

"Is that Christopher Columbus?" she whispered to Carlos.

"No, that's the captain of one of his ships. Admiral Columbus wants everyone on board before midnight."

"Why?"

"That's the deadline, remember?" Carlos said. "Many of the crewmen are like me—*conversos*. It is safer if they go."

Heather bit her lip. Would it be safer for Carlos to go, too? She climbed over and sat beside him, studying his face. Was this all some grand scheme for him to escape? Maybe he really wasn't here to deliver a message at all.

Hadn't he said she was on her own after Palos? The thought sent a sudden shiver down her spine.

"What about me, Carlos?" she said. "Where will I be safe?"

"Here in Spain?" Carlos shrugged. "I do not know."

"Help me go with Columbus, then. It's my only way out." Her mind raced to come up with a plan. "Tell him I'm a good worker, that Queen Isabella sent me. You could add a postscript to their message."

Carlos shook his head as he retrieved a parchment scroll. "It bears the royal mark, you see? I cannot open it without breaking the seal."

On inspecting the wax imprint, Heather's hopes sank. "Still," she pleaded, "couldn't you try to convince him?"

"One girl among forty men? *Imposible, niña!*"

"What if I cut my hair and dressed as a boy? Oh, please, Carlos! If I stay, I'll surely be caught and . . . and killed."

Carlos touched her cheek gently and sighed. "I've an extra tunic and breeches in the back. See if you can make them fit." He jumped down from the wagon, the sealed message in his hand. "When I give this to the admiral, I'll do what I can."

"*Gracias,* Carlos. And would you hold this for safekeeping?" He nodded as she handed over the noisy string of gold coins that Señor Vargas had given her. "If this works . . ." She broke off, mustering a grateful smile. "Good luck!" As if she were reinforcing her words, she touched the *chai* necklace beneath her robe.

Carlos doffed his cap and saluted her. "*Viva Heather!*"— "May you live long, Heather."

She held her breath, watching him go. Finally, she went to the back of the wagon to change into his extra clothes. She had just taken off her necklace and hooded robe when Carlos's horse whinnied shrilly. Instinctively, she made a grab for the gold charm.

When she looked up, it was into the eyes of an armed guard—then into the bright, axlike blade of his halberd.

"What do you have there, young gypsy?" he sneered. "Open your hand."

Heather backed away, squeezing the charm so tightly that it pricked her palm. She tried to scream for Carlos, but her voice, her very breath, failed her. In a heartbeat she knew that the stranger's well-polished weapon would be the last thing she'd ever see.

C h a p t e r

Seven

QUESTIONS WITHOUT ANSWERS

s the guard reached for Heather, she trained her gaze on his wide, upraised blade. All she got was a glimpse of the shiny, mirrorlike surface. Clutching her necklace and closing her eyes, she prayed it was enough.

With her heart pounding in her ears, Heather forced herself to look. She was safe again in Ellie's attic! A grateful breath whooshed out of her as she sank to her knees on the oriental rug. When she finally unclenched her fist, her necklace had imprinted a *chai* on her palm.

For a long while, Heather sat there, too stunned and exhausted to move. Then, without warning, her eyes welled with tears. I survived the Spanish Inquisition, she thought. But how many people didn't? She couldn't help wondering about Carlos. Had he signed on with Columbus and escaped to the New World? Perhaps he'd stayed—and lived with the fear that his new faith would be questioned, that one unsuspecting day he, too, would be put to death. Heather only wished there'd been a way to let him know she was safe.

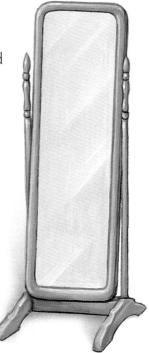

And what of the Vargas family and her own ancestors, the Jardins? Had they made it to Turkey? When had they come to America and changed the family name to Hardin? All at once, it seemed terribly important to Heather that she know and honor the memory of those who had gone before her. That she remember, that she never forget. Maybe she'd even study her family genealogy the way Keisha had studied hers, or at least start paying better attention in temple school.

"Omigosh!" At the thought of her friend, Heather jumped to her feet and quickly changed out of the gypsy outfit and into her clothes. What time was it? She peered out the window. The sun was already painting the western sky. If she didn't hurry, she'd be late for the seder. With a start, she realized that she was actually looking forward to it.

The seder plate with all its special foods had the place of honor in the center of the Hardins' festive dining table. All eyes were on Heather's father as he opened the big velvet-covered book. "This is called the Haggadah," he explained to her friends. "It contains all the rituals of Passover—prayers, poetry, songs, and especially the story of how the Israelites escaped Pharaoh's slavery."

Keisha's eyes met Heather's for a moment, and the two exchanged a knowing smile. Different stories but the same somehow, Heather thought. Definitely worth telling—and hearing again and again.

"If you girls don't

mind," Mr. Hardin continued, "we'll pass the book around and take turns reading."

Heather listened to the story with new ears and heard with a new heart. Through it she relived her adventure in Spain—the hurried departure, the hard journey, the hope of freedom. When it was her turn to read, her voice caught with emotion.

Grandma Hardin reached over and patted Heather's hand. Her dad raised a questioning eyebrow at her mother.

Finally, Heather reached the end of her section and passed the book to Grandma Hardin. She realized then that everyone seemed to be staring at her. "What?" she said. "Do I have toothpaste on my face?"

Megan and Alison giggled.

"Not hardly," Jenna said. "It's just—"

"The way you were reading," Keisha broke in. "Really getting into it—you know, like you were there or something. It was so cool!"

"Now how could I be in ancient Egypt?" Heather asked.

Beneath the table, someone—Megan or Alison— kicked her in reply. Their frozen expressions across the way seemed to say, "*We* know. You went through the mirror, didn't you? Tell us everything!"

Heather shrugged mysteriously. They'd just have to

wait. There were still the Four Questions to ask
and answer, as well as the symbolic dipping and spilling
and hand washing and tears. There was still dinner to
eat and Grandma Hardin's other present to open. But
after that, Heather would tell them. It was the Magic
Attic Club's only rule.

Chapter

Eight

LOST AND FOUND

hen Heather rose to clear the dinner dishes, Keisha jumped up to help. Megan and Alison joined in, too. The three girls cornered Heather in the kitchen. "So?" Keisha prompted. "You went to the attic, didn't you?"

"What did you try on?" asked Megan.

"Where did you go?" Alison chimed in.

Heather grinned. "I promise. I'll tell you everything, only—"

"Girls," Mr. Hardin called from the dining room. "Time to find the *afikomen*."

"The Africa men?" Keisha giggled.

"No," Heather said. "The ah-fi-KO-men. The middle matzoh. Daddy hides the second one from the stack, and whoever finds it gets a prize."

"Cool." Alison's blue eyes danced. "Come on, before Jenna beats us to it."

Heather watched her friends race for the dining room and grinned. Who would have guessed that they'd all have so much fun?

"Okay, Mr. H., here we are," Alison announced. "Do you say 'On your mark, get set, go!' or what?"

Heather's father laughed. "Not quite. First, I explain the rules—"

"Rules, shmules," Grandma Hardin cut in. "Let the *afikomen* wait. First, we open my present." Heather's father didn't argue, so she turned to Jenna. "Will you hand me that box behind you, dear? Careful now. Don't drop it."

The girls drew closer. Grandma Hardin passed the box to her son. "I think you should open it, Jeremy," she said, watching him intently.

Heather held her breath as her father separated the layers of tissue paper. With a frown, he looked up at his mother.

"What is it, Dad?" Heather rose on tiptoe, but couldn't get even a glimpse.

"I . . . I'm not sure."

As her father lifted a squat, brown shape from the box, icy fingers seemed to squeeze the back of Heather's neck. With a shiver, she strained to see.

"Gee, Mama, this is most . . . unusual." Mr. Hardin set the pitiful excuse for a vase on the table and glanced at Heather's mother. "Have you ever seen anything quite like it, Sarah?"

"No, never."

I have, Heather wanted to say. It's just like Señora Vargas's! "Grandma," she asked instead, "may I hold it? I promise I'll be careful."

Her grandmother nodded, and Keisha, Alison, and Megan inched even closer to Heather. "It sure looks old," Megan said.

"Right you are!" Grandma Hardin's eyes glowed as if she'd just received a compliment. "And it's finally back in the family where it belongs."

"Where was it, Grandma?" Jenna asked.

"Missing for at least a generation, dear. But I took up the search where your grandpa left off, and just last month got word from a museum in Canada. . . ." She shook her head. "Too bad he never lived to see its secrets."

"Secrets?" Heather's stomach rose and fell. Señora Vargas had never said anything about *her* vase having secrets, had she?

Grandma Hardin shrugged apologetically. "All he told me was that somehow this old vase had kept his family together since the days of Columbus. I'm sorry, Heather. I wish I knew more."

Lifting it higher, Heather examined the bottom. Still puzzled, she turned it over in her hands. Something clicked faintly. "What was that?" she asked, but no one else seemed to have heard. She rotated the vase a second time. *Fffft.* The strange sound came again!

Something was definitely in there. But when Heather peered inside, the vase was empty. Frustrated, she ran her fingers like a blind person's over the surface. Was that a crack? she wondered. Or part of the design? Her pulse quickened as she twisted the base.

"Omigosh!" Heather gasped as the vase opened. Nestled inside were tiny replicas of the same Jewish objects she had seen in her own home: a Kiddush cup to hold

wine for the Sabbath and holiday prayers, a Chanukah menorah, a spice box, and many others. They included everything a person would need to secretly celebrate the Sabbath and other Jewish holidays. Heather's hand trembled as she withdrew each fragile connection with the *familia* Jardin. Here was proof that they had kept their faith. "Grandma, look!"

Her grandmother's eyes shone with sudden tears.

"This is amazing, Mama," Heather's father said, and quickly explained the significance of Heather's discovery.

Everyone murmured as Heather set the vase carefully on the table. Grandma Hardin fingered the miniatures in awe. "I never thought I'd see this day," she said.

Heather turned to hug her grandmother. As she did, she caught sight of her friends' excited faces. "Me, either, Grandma," she whispered. At last, she pulled away and, with a mischievous grin at Alison, Megan, and Keisha, made a dash for the living room. "Come on, girls," she called, "time to find the *afikomen!*"

Diary

Dear Diary,

I can't believe that I haven't had time to write all week. You'll never guess what Grandma and I have been doing—recording a family history.

Ever since I dressed up as a gypsy and went through the mirror, I've been dying to hear everything Grandma knows about our Spanish ancestors — where they went, how they survived. It kind of makes me feel bad that I never really made time to listen to all her stories before. That's all they were then—stories. Now, they're <u>histories.</u>

Being on the run in Spain sure gave me a different feeling about Passover, too. We left for Sevilla in such a hurry that if Señora Vargas had been making bread, she'd never have been able to let it rise. We'd have ended up with matzoh, just like in the seder story! When you live through something like that, you want to make sure that it never happens again. Passover helps us remember, and I can finally see why that's important.

Did I tell you who found the afikomen? It was Megan. And no wonder. Dad hid it inside one of Mom's art books on the coffee table! Her prize was a five-dollar bill, and on Sunday she took the whole Magic Attic Club out for ice cream.

Today was my last day of eating breadless lunches, but you know what? I wasn't alone. Keisha, Megan, and Alison have decided that peanut butter and jelly on matzoh tastes a lot better than it looks!

Luv,

Heather

Learn
More
About It

HISTORICAL
NOTE

ews first sailed to the Iberian (Spanish) peninsula
from the Middle East at least 1,000 years before
the current calendar came into use. Even Jonah in
the Bible is said to have traveled to Cádiz, Spain. These
Spanish, or Sephardic Jews claimed a proud history and
felt superior to Jews from other countries. They flourished
and lived in peace among their neighbors for centuries—
that is until 1492, one of the most important times in all
of Spain's long history.

Until that year, the country was under the rule of the
Moors, Arab conquerors from the Mideast. With the
defeat of the last Moorish ruler of the kingdom of
Granada that January, the entire country was finally
united under King Ferdinand and Queen Isabella. To
bring the people together even more, they wanted the
Jews and Arabs who lived in southern Spain to give up
their own religious beliefs and to convert to Catholicism,
the rulers' faith. In an official decree issued at the end of
March, all Jews were ordered to convert or to leave Spain

by midnight on August 2, 1492. Ten years later, Moors would be given the same agonizing choice.

During this period, there were many high-ranking Jewish advisers in the royal court. Some changed their family names and their religion in order to stay in Spain. The fictional character Carlos Nuñez comes from such a family. Others—like Queen Isabella's brilliant financial aide, Don Isaac Abravanel—refused to convert and fled the country. Interestingly, he and other Jewish advisers were largely responsible for convincing Queen Isabella to support Christopher Columbus and for providing much of the financing for his voyage.

Those Jews who appeared to accept the rulers' faith were often called *Marranos*, a slang expression meaning "pigs." If they remained secret Jews, as the fictional Vargas family did, they were always in danger of being reported to the Inquisition—the very harsh and cruel tribunal that investigated charges of heresy—and put to death. Washing one's hands too often or using a clean tablecloth on the wrong day was considered proof of their guilt. The "vase of secrets" was actually used by *Marranos* to keep their Jewish faith alive, and replicas still exist.

Many historians believe it is no coincidence that Christopher Columbus sailed from Palos the day after all Jews were expelled from Spain. Using maps and technology created by Jews and a crew that included many recent converts, Columbus may well have had personal reasons for setting sail on August 3. One noted Spanish historian is convinced that Columbus was descended from a Jewish family that converted and then moved to Italy. Unfortunately, the records and journals that would have put to rest all doubts about the explorer's own ancestry disappeared after his death.

GLOSSARY OF SPANISH TERMS

a sus órdenes (*ah soos* OR-*then-ess*) literally, at your orders. An expression used upon meeting someone, in much the same way that "glad to meet you" is used.

Alhambra (*all-*HAHM-*brah*) the palace and fortress of the Moorish kings of Granada, built in the 13th-14th centuries; occupied on occasion by King Ferdinand and Queen Isabella after the fall of Granada in January, 1492

aquí (*ah-*KEE) here

buenas tardes (BWAY-*nahs* TAR-*thayss*) good afternoon

cálmate (CAHL-*mah-tay*) calm yourself

chica (CHEEK-*ah*) young girl; also means small

ciega (*see-*AY-*gah*) blind girl or woman

comprendo (*kohm-*PREND-*thoh*) I understand

conversos (*kohn-*VAIR-*sohss*) converts

dueña (DWAYN-*yah*) chaperone

espére (*ess-*PAIR-*ay*) wait

est·s (*ess*-TAHSS) you are; (when used in a question: are you)

familia (*fah*-MEEL-*yah*) family

gracias (GRAH-*see-ahss*) thank you

Granada (*grah*-NAH-*thah*) city and province in southern Spain that was conquered by King Ferdinand and Queen Isabella in January, 1492

hijo (EE-*hoh*) son

imposible (*eem-poh*-SEE-*blay*) impossible

jardín (*har*-DEEN) garden

Mamá (*mah*-MAH) Mommy; affectionate term for mother

mañana (*mahn*-YAH-*nah*) tomorrow

maravedís (*mar-ah-vay*-DEESS) the standard unit for measuring monetary value during Queen Isabella's reign. In the late 15th century, a common laborer would earn 15 to 20 maravedis a day. A carpenter or mason would earn about 40. The 19-carat gold coin called a dobla was worth 445 maravedis.

me llamo (*may* YAH-*moh*) my name is

mira (MEE-*rah*) look

momento; un momento (*oon moh*-MEN-*toh*) moment; a moment

nada más que (NAH-*thah mahss kay*) merely (literally, nothing more than)

niña (NEEN-*yah*) female child

no lo sé (*no low say*) I don't know it

nunca (NOON-*kah*) never

Papá (*pah*-PAH) Daddy; affectionate term for father

perdida (*pair*-THEE-*thah*) lost

perdón (*pair*-THOHN) pardon, forgiveness

por qué (*pohr kay*) why (literally, for what)

porque (*pohr*-KAY) because

prima (PREE-*mah*) female cousin

Sacromonte (*sah-crow*-MOHN-*tay*) literally, Holy Mountain; the mountain opposite the Alhambra where for centuries gypsies have lived in hillside caves

sé (*say*) I know

señor (*sen*-YOR) mister; a man

señora (*sen*-YOR-*ah*) missus; a married woman

sí (*see*) yes

viva (VEE-*vah*) long live; hurrah (a cry of exclamation)

JOIN THE MAGIC ATTIC CLUB!

You can enjoy every adventure of the Magic Attic Club just by reading all the books. And there's more!

You can have a whole world of fun with the dolls, outfits, and accessories that are based on the books. And since Alison, Keisha, Heather, and Megan can wear one another's clothes, you can relive their adventures, or create new ones of your own!

To join the Magic Attic Club, just fill out this postcard and drop it in the mail, or call toll free **1-800-221-6972**. We'll send you a **free** membership kit

including a poster, bookmark, postcards, and a catalog with all four dolls.

With your first purchase of a doll, you'll also receive your own key to the attic. And it's FREE!

Yes, I want to join the Magic Attic Club!

My name is _____

My address is _____

City _____ State _____ Zip _____

Birth date _____ Parent's Signature _____

955

And send a catalog to my friend, too!

My friend's name is _____

Address _____

City _____ State _____ Zip _____

956

If someone has already used the postcard from
this book and you would like a free Magic Attic Club
catalog, just send your full name and address to:

Magic Attic Club
866 Spring Street
P.O. Box 9712
Portland, ME 04104-9954

Or call toll free
1-800-775-9272

Code: 957
